The WONDERFUL WORLD of OZ

For Jonny and Wilson, who make our house a home – M.M.

For the staff and children of

Osbaston Church in Wales School – S.H.

EGMONT

We bring stories to life

The Wonderful Wizard of Oz by L. Frank Baum first published in 1900.
This original picture book adaptation first published in 2018 under the title *The Wizard of Oz*, by Egmont UK Limited
The Yellow Building, 1 Nicholas Road, London W11 4AN

www.egmont.co.uk

Text copyright © Sam Hay 2018
Illustrations copyright © Meg McLaren 2018
Adaptation based on character designs created by Meg McLaren

The moral rights of the authors and illustrator have been asserted.

ISBN 978 1 4052 8629 9

The WIZARD of OZ

Based on the original story by **L. Frank Baum**

Adapted by **Meg McLaren** and **Sam Hay**

EGMONT

Once upon a windswept prairie
lived Little Dot and her dog, Toto.

They dreamed of
exciting adventures.

Dot's
(NOT F
JA

So when a strange swirly-whirly, hurly-burly wind came howling by one day, they just knew something extraordinary was about to happen.

Little Dot's auntie didn't like the wild wind. She knew it meant big trouble.

"Run inside!" she shouted. "There's a tornado coming!"

But as Little Dot and Toto
ran into the house –

Whoosh!

The tornado whisked up
the house and blew it
far, **far** away.

Up, **up** it flew.
Up into the sky.

Then **down,**
down – **bump!**

Thump!

The house had landed in
a strange and beautiful land . . .

Where little people dressed in blue were cheering:
"**Hooray**, you've squished the Bad Witch!"

Little Dot didn't know what they were talking about, until . . .

...oops! She spotted two sparkly silver boots, poking out from under her house.

A lady in a starry cloak stepped forward. "I am the Good Witch from the North," she said. "The Bad Witch you squashed has a sister, the Even Worse Witch, and she'll be very cross with you. You'd better go home."

But Little Dot didn't know the way home.
"What will we do?" she said.

"Follow the yellow brick road to the Emerald City and see the
Wonderful Wizard of Oz. He will help you get home,"
the Good Witch suggested.

EMERALD CITY

"And put the Bad Witch's
silver boots on – they're magic
and might be useful!"

"Thank you,"
Little Dot said.

Then she took a deep breath.
"Come on, Toto, let's go
find our way home."

And they set off on their big adventure.

They hadn't gone far along the yellow brick road,
when they found a worried-looking lion.

"I'm s-s-s-scared," he wailed.
"I've just seen a t-t-t-talking
scarecrow!"

Little Dot was about to explain that
scarecrows couldn't talk, when –

"Hi!" the scarecrow said.

Toto woofed. But Little Dot just giggled. "How can you talk?"

Scarecrow didn't know. "You see, I haven't got a **brain** to think with," he said.

Little Dot had an idea. "Let's ask the Wonderful Wizard of Oz to give you a brain. He can do **anything**!"

"Could he make me **braver**, too?"
Lion sniffled.

"**Of course,**"
Little Dot said.

So they all set off together, taking care
to follow the **yellow brick road**.

And all the while keeping watch
for the Even Worse Witch!

Soon they came to a bridge. They were about to cross when Toto's paws started to slip and slide and he nearly skidded off the side!

"Watch out," said a little tin can. "I was oiling the bridge when I sneezed and I couldn't be bothered to clean up the mess."

Little Dot frowned.
"That wasn't very kind."

"I don't know how to be kind," Tin Can said. "I have no heart."

Little Dot knew who could help.
"Let's ask the Wonderful Wizard of Oz
to give you a heart."

But first they'd have to cross the oily bridge.
Luckily, Scarecrow had a plan. He laid his coat over the puddle.

But when they reached
the other side . . .

...boo!

It was the Even Worse Witch!
She had been waiting to jump out at them.

Toto began to bark. Little Dot's friends were t-e-r-r-i-f-i-e-d!
But Little Dot wasn't scared.
"Don't you frighten my friends," she scolded.

The Even Worse Witch stuck out her tongue,
then waggled her wand.

The yellow brick road began to
quake and shake and then . . .

...hissss! Ginormous jelly snakes came slithering up through the cracks in the road.

Lion **leapt** in front of his friends.

ROAR!

The snakes were SO scared, they melted!

The Even Worse Witch
was **hopping mad** now.
She waggled her wand again
and a big cloud of
boiled sweets appeared.

"Quick! Hide behind me,"
Tin Can said, and the sweets
pinged off his tummy.

The Even Worse Witch's face turned purple
with rage. She raised her wand again . . .

"Uh-oh!" said Little Dot.

But just then Toto pawed
at Little Dot's
backpack.

"Of course," Little Dot said,
"my packed lunch!" and she
whipped out a yoghurt.

She shook it.
And shook it!
And – splat!
She squirted it
at the witch.

"Ahhh!"
shrieked the witch.
"You've ruined
my best frock!"
She was so
angry she –

POPPED!

Gone.
Forever.

"Hooray for
Little Dot and Toto!"
Scarecrow shouted.

Little Dot hugged
her friends tight.

"Let's go find
**The Wonderful
Wizard of Oz!**"
cheered Tin Can.

And they raced down the yellow brick road,
all the way to the wizard's palace in the **Emerald City.**

And waiting inside was a kindly old gentleman –

The Wonderful Wizard of Oz!

Little Dot's friends were too shy to speak.
But Little Dot wasn't. She told him **everything**.

The Wonderful Wizard of Oz
listened carefully. Then he smiled
and said: "You don't need my help."

And he reminded Scarecrow about his
brainy idea to cross the oily bridge.

ROAR!

And how **brave** Lion had been
with the jelly snakes.

And how Tin Can had so kindly
shielded his friends from the sweets,
so he already had a **heart**.

Then he gave each of them a sticker for good work. The friends **beamed** with pride.

"I'm so proud of you," Little Dot said, hugging her friends tight.

But she still hadn't got the answer to **her** problem.

"How will I get home?" she asked, sadly.

The wizard smiled.
"You had the answer all along."
He pointed to her
silver boots.

"Knock your heels together
three times and think of home."

Little Dot picked up Toto,
and thought of her auntie.

Knock!

Knock!

Knock!

The boots began to
shimmer and sparkle!

And in the **wink** of an eye,
Little Dot and Toto were . . .

. . . home!

And their house was back too!

Little Dot's auntie swept them up in a huge hug.

"We've had the best adventure and made lots of new friends," said Little Dot as she snuggled in. "But I'm so glad to be home."